TERRY
AND THE
EARTHQUAKE
by MIKE RUCKER

Another adventure in the *Terry the Tractor™* Series

FIRST EDITION

UNIVERSITY EDITIONS, Inc.
c/o Mike Rucker
1003 W. Centennial Dr.
Peoria, IL 61614-2828

Cover and interior art by Bob Burchett

"We are one. Our cause is one. And we must
help each other if we are to succeed."
— *Frederick Douglass*

Dedication

For Zack and Drew

*Thanks for editing and proofreading to Yvonne Frey
and Ross Gidcumb of Peoria, Illinois and to
Sherry Seckler of Peoria for the music composition.*

**An excavator and an articulated
dump truck working on a rock job.**

The boss called the machines together to tell them about their new job.

"We have a very difficult job to tackle and we will have to work together as a team. You must work together to build a new highway through these very rocky mountains. Each team member will have a special job to do," he told the machines.

The boss continued, "This job will involve a lot of 'cuts' and 'fills'. Do you all know about cuts and fills?"

"Yes," answered Terry. "In a 'cut' we cut down into the ground – or, down into the rock at this job site. Then trucks or scrapers haul the dirt or rock away."

"That's right, Terry." The boss said. "And who can explain a 'fill' to me?"

Timmy Truck spoke up, "A fill is where I dump the dirt and rocks from the cut."

The boss nodded his head in approval and said, "Correct, Timmy."

The boss continued, "Now here are your assigned jobs: Travis Tractor's job is to use his ripper to break up hard rock in the cut."

The other machines glanced at the ripper on the back of Travis' frame. It was sort of like a long tooth. It could cut into the hard rock like a big knife.

The boss then turned to Exeter Excavator, "Your job will be to load the broken rock into Timmy Truck. Timmy will haul the rock and dump it on the fill."

"What is my job?" asked Terry.

The boss said, "Terry, because there are only four of you to start this project you will have two responsibilities."

"That's great!" Terry said. "I like to stay busy. What are my two jobs?"

The boss answered, "Your first job is to use your bulldozer to make piles of the rock which Travis rips up. That will make it easier for Exeter to load it into Timmy."

"I can do that really well," Terry told the boss. "What is my second job?"

"For your second job you must occasionally leave the cut and go over to the fill. There you must spread the rock that Timmy dumps on the fill. Then you must compact it with your tracks to make a smooth surface for the road to be built," the boss answered.

"I can do all that," Terry told the boss.

"I know you can, Terry," the boss replied, "You are a good worker. But as soon as possible I will get another team member, a special machine to compact the rock on the fill.

"What does that word, 'compact' mean?" asked Timmy.

Terry answered, "It means packing down the rock and dirt to make a hard and smooth surface for the road to be built."

"That's right," the boss told the machines.

Soon the four machines were hard at work.

"We're the greatest team that ever was," shouted Travis Tractor as he pulled his ripper to break up the tough rock.

"Yeah," said Timmy, "we've got great team spirit."

Travis and the other machines were certainly working as team.

Occasionally, after Timmy had dumped several loads of broken rock, Terry dashed over to the fill. There he spread the broken rock with his bulldozer. Then he ran back and forth over the fill. He used his steel tracks to compact the rock. Because he had two jobs to do, Terry had trouble keeping up with the work. Sometimes when he had to leave the cut to do some compacting on the fill, Exeter would not have enough broken rock to load into Timmy.

The energetic machines all liked each other and worked together as hard as they could. The other machines knew that Terry was working extra hard because he had two different duties. Terry was very proud that he had two important jobs to do.

One day a pack of wolves happened by. The wolf pack leader stopped to speak to the machines. "Hi," he said, "I'm Wiley Wolf. I'm the leader of this great team of wolves."

"We're a great team, too," Terry told Wiley. "We're a terrific road building team. Why is your wolf pack a good team?"

Wiley responded, "We're great because we hunt well together. By hunting as a team we can get a lot more food than if we each hunted alone." Also, he continued, "We are a great singing team. Listen!" And all the wolves raised their heads and joined in a great howling song: "Owww, owwww, owwwww!"

"Does that song mean anything?" Travis asked?

"Yes," Wiley Wolf answered, "It means that we are the greatest wolf pack team around.

The wolf pack began to sing again. All the wolves, young and old, raised their heads to the sky and howled their special song.

HI, I'M WILEY WOLF LEADER OF THIS TEAM OF WOLVES
WE ARE A GREAT TEAM TOO

Just as they were finishing the song, two young wolf pups began to fuss with each other.

Wiley was strict with the two pups, " Wilbur and Wilford, stop that! I have had enough of your bickering."

But the two young wolves continued to fight. They nipped at each other until one bit the ear of the other very hard. The injured pup cried loudly and came running to Wiley for protection. He tried to hide behind Wiley as the other pup came running after him.

"Why are they fighting?" Terry asked Wiley.

"They are being very silly," Wiley answered. "They each claim they can sing better than the other, so they fight about it. They are not yet good team members."

Wilbur yelped, "I am a better singer than Wilford. He is always off key."

"No, I am not," howled Wilford. "I can sing louder and better than you any day." He nipped at Wilbur's nose.

"Look, kids!" Wiley snapped at them. "I have had enough of your silly rivalry. You are both good singers. The pack needs both of you. Now learn to get along with each other."

The pups quieted down and Wiley said to the machines, "Those two do not yet know how to be good team members. They each want to be better than the other. They have to learn that they are equally important to the team."

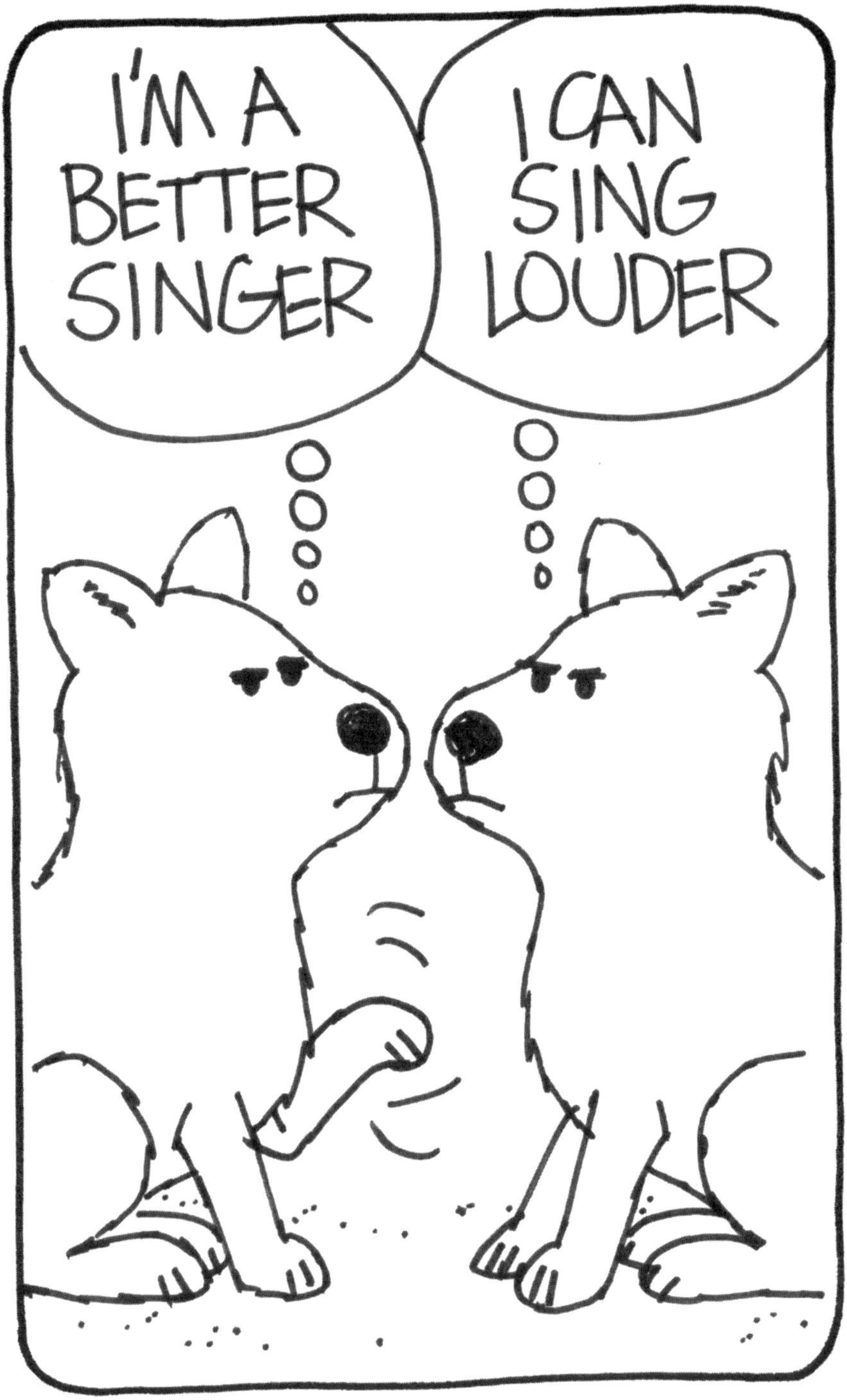
I'M A BETTER SINGER
I CAN SING LOUDER

To change the subject, Terry asked, "Do you have any other songs?"

"Yes, we do have some other songs, such as this one." And then Wiley and the others howled a different song. It was more of a yipping song that sounded very strange and urgent: "Yip yip yip oww! yip yip oww!"

"What does that song mean?" Terry asked.

"That is our warning song," Wiley answered. "It means there is danger. We use it when we are concerned and want to tell others that something is wrong. We do not sing it often, only when we are worried about something."

Wiley and the others in his pack told the machines that they had to go, so the new friends, wolves and machines, said goodbye to each other.

As the wolves left, Terry noticed that Wilbur and Wilford were still nipping at each other.

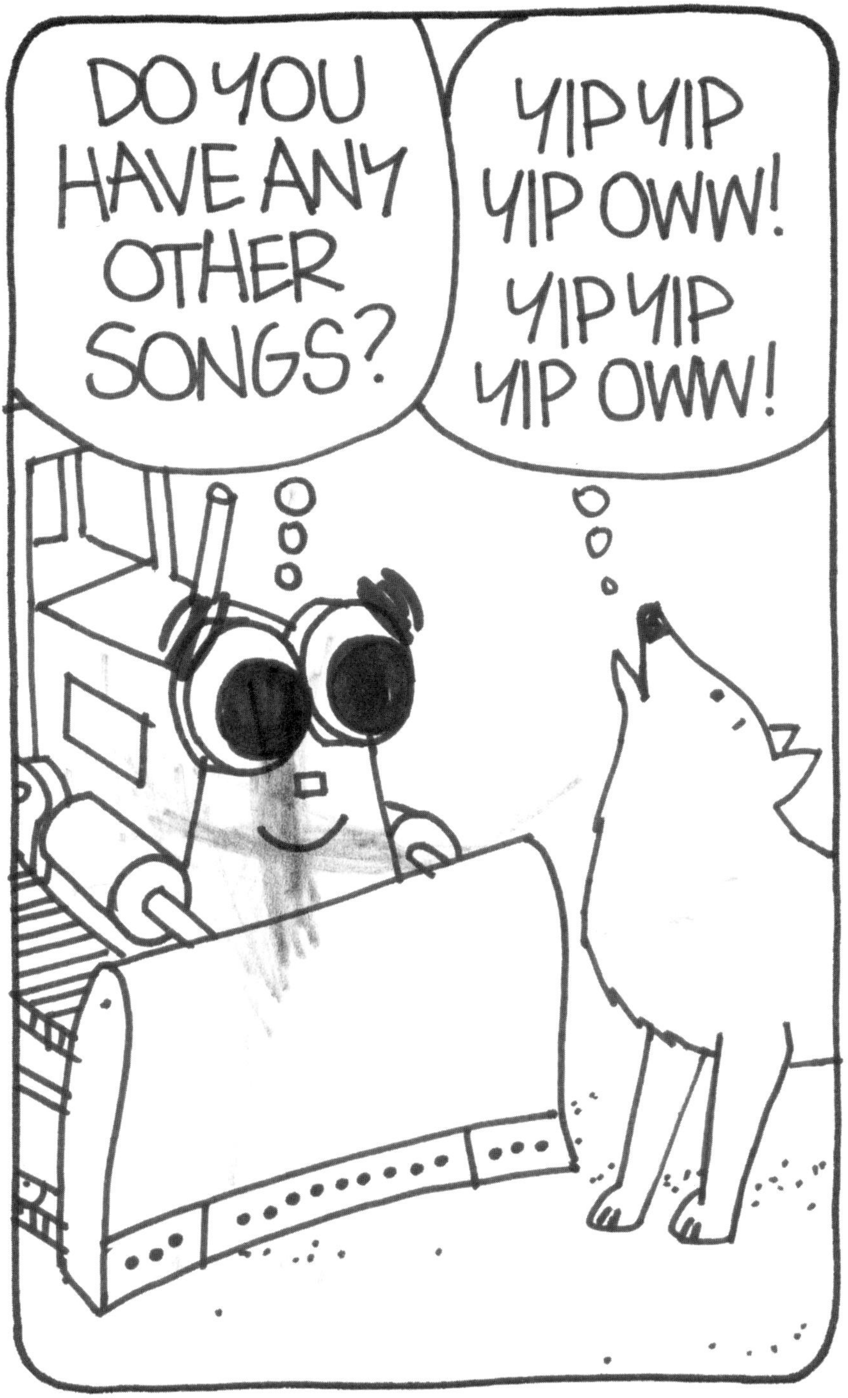
DO YOU HAVE ANY OTHER SONGS?
YIP YIP YIP OWW! YIP YIP YIP OWW!

The boss came to see the machines. "You guys are doing a good job," he told them. "But we need some help for Terry. Terry, as I told you earlier, we needed another team member. Now we need you to work full time using your bulldozer. The work will go faster if you do not have to do the compacting as well as the bulldozing."

"But," Terry protested, "someone has to compact the fill. I use my tracks to do that job." "Yes," the boss answered, "but the team needs you to do the bulldozing. Your tracks are not the best tool to do the compacting job. Also your tracks will wear out very fast when you use them to compact rock. I have found a new team player who is available to do that job. Here he comes now."

The machines looked up and saw a new machine coming onto the job site. It was a compactor machine with large steel wheels. Each wheel had many knobs to crush and compact the dirt and rocks. There was also a bulldozer on the front of the machine.

As the new machine rolled off the trailer, the boss said, "Let me introduce Calib the Compactor."

Calib flashed his headlight eyes and said, "Hi, Dudes. I'm Calib the Colossal. I'm the greatest compactor in the business."

In addition to his flashy steel wheels Calib had a special paint job with racing stripes and flames.

The other machines looked at each other. They were not sure they wanted the flashy Calib on their team.

"Hello," Terry said "I'm pleased to meet you." But, Terry was telling a fib. He had decided right away that he did not like Calib – and he did not want him on the team taking over part of his job.

The other machines also said, "Hello" to Calib, but none said it in a really friendly way.

"Okay," the boss said. "Let's get back to work. Terry you stay in the cut to do the bulldozing. I'll get Calib started on the compacting work on the fill."

The work now went along faster because Terry had to do only his dozing job while Calib did the compacting job. Calib began spreading the broken rock on the fill. Then he ran over the rocks with his steel wheels to compact the fill so the road could be built. Terry and the other machines saw that Calib did a better job than Terry had been able to do. This was because Calib had his special steel wheels that were made to do that job. Terry's tracks were not made for that job. Terry felt bad that Calib could do a better job with the compacting than he could.

All the machines were doing a good job with their special skills. Calib was a good addition to the team, but he made the other machines angry because he sometimes told them how good he was. "I'm the greatest compactor in the world," he often said. "See how smooth I can make the fill with my super steel wheels. I'm the greatest."

Calib was certainly good at his special skill, but his bragging made the other team members dislike him.

After work one day Terry told Travis, "I cannot stand Calib's bragging. He makes me mad." Travis told Terry that he felt the same way.

Larry and Timmy were nearby and they agreed with the tractors that Calib was not very pleasant to be with. But Timmy told the others, "He really is good at his job. I think we just have to put up with him. His bragging does not hurt us."

Calib came near and called out, "Hey guys. Are you having a meeting? What's up?" The other machines ignored Calib and went back to work. Calib felt bad because he knew the other machines did not like him.

The boss noticed that Calib was irritating the other machines with his bragging. The boss took him aside and said, "Calib, you do very good work, but you must be more of a team player. You have to consider how your boasting affects the others in the team."

Calib thought about the situation. He now realized that his bragging caused the others to dislike him. He decided to continue to do his job well but also to be nice to the others. He wanted the others to be his friends.

Even though Calib changed his ways and did not brag any more, Terry and Travis still did not like him. They often told each other how much they disliked the compactor.

One day Terry was feeling grumpy. He decided that he just could not stand working with Calib another day. He told Travis, "I'm going to quit this job. The boss will just have to find another tractor to do my bulldozing job."

Travis responded, "Terry, I agree that Calib is not easy to like, but he does a good job. I don't want you to go. If I can put up with Calib, you can too."

But Terry was very irritable that day. When the boss came to the job site, Terry announced to him that he was going to quit because he did not like working with Calib.

The boss was surprised and upset with Terry. "You mean you want to break up this good team just because you do not like another team member? Terry, that is selfish and thoughtless."

The boss told Terry, "The mark of a great team is not that all the players are compatible. The important thing is how well they handle incompatibility."

"What does that mean?" Terry asked.

The boss answered, "It means that you do not have to like every member of your team. If one does a good job the other team members should work with him. You should not let your personal feelings get in the way of good team performance." He continued, "Terry, this is a great team. Don't you want to be a part of it?"

"Well, yes," Terry answered, rather ashamed. "I just don't like that Calib with all of his bragging."

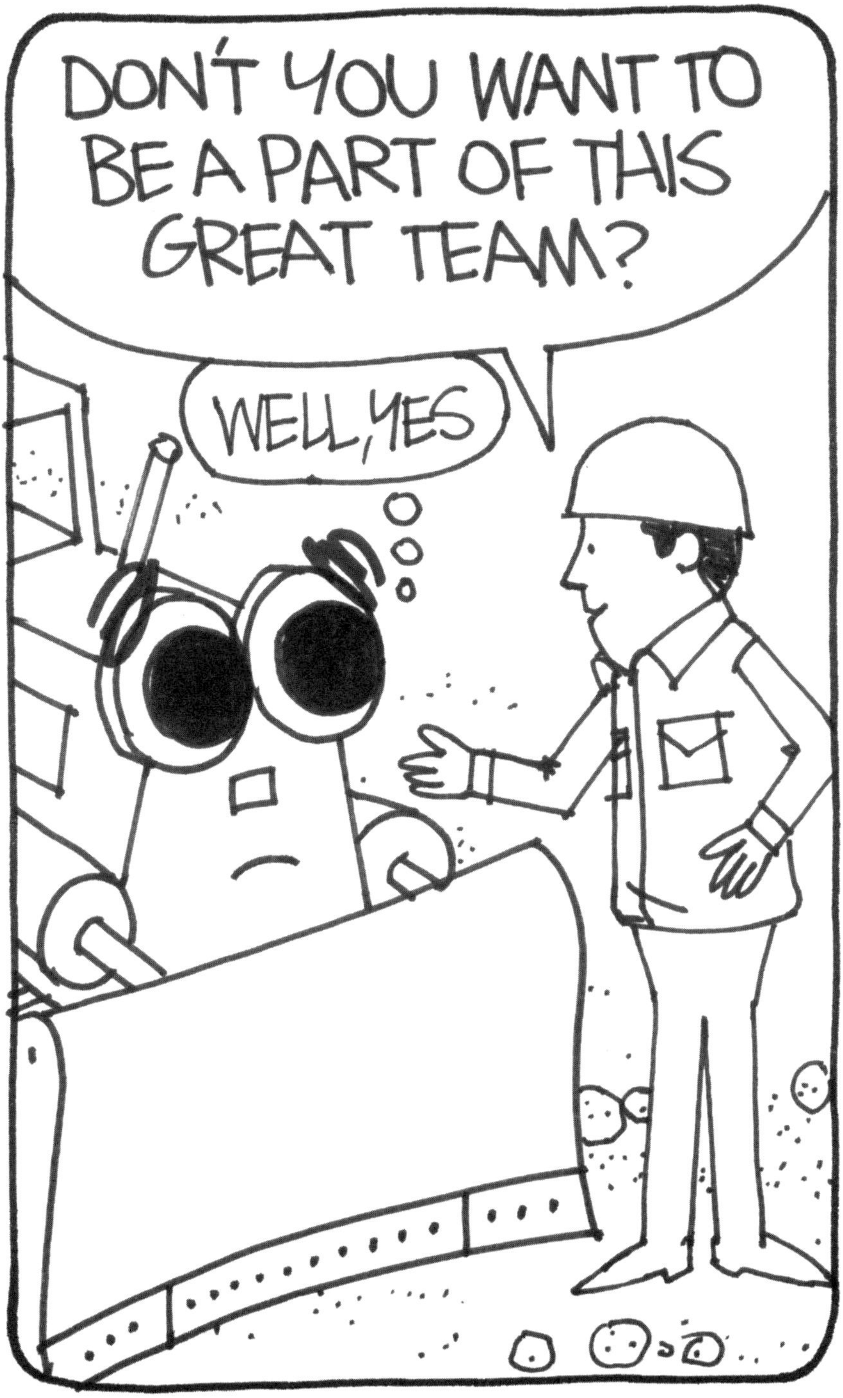
DON'T YOU WANT TO BE A PART OF THIS GREAT TEAM?
WELL, YES

The boss told him, "Terry, sometimes getting along with others can be the hardest part of a job."

Terry said, "I just want to do a good job. I know that Calib does a good job as a compactor, but I try to do a good job with my bulldozer."

The boss continued, "Yes, Terry, you are good with your bulldozer, but you are not yet a good team player. Being a good team player is a very important part of the job. I have talked with Calib about his bragging and he has agreed to stop it. Now, Terry, it is up to you to make some changes."

"How do you want me to change?" Terry asked.

"Terry, you need to change your attitude. You can change the way you feel about Calib. Think about this, Terry. Calib has become a better team player, while you have become less of a team member because you do not like him."

This made Terry feel very bad. He was ashamed to think that Calib was a better team player than himself. He began to cry. He sobbed, "I think I will just quit this job. I don't want to be a poor team player."

The boss replied, "Terry, quitting is not the way to solve this problem. If you want to feel good about yourself, you must change your attitude. You cannot change Calib. You must change yourself. You may take off work for the rest of the day to think about this. If you decide to quit tomorrow, that will be your own decision. But I hope you will decide to stay as part of this team. We all need you."

Terry went away where he could be alone and think about what the boss had said. He knew the boss was right. He knew he had to change his attitude. He was still feeling very ashamed of himself, when he heard Wiley and the other wolves howling.

At first Terry was glad the wolves were nearby. He hoped they would come to see him. Then Terry noticed that the song they were singing was their special danger song: "Yip yip yip oww! yip yip oww!" That worried Terry. He wondered what was wrong.

Terry decided to go to look for the wolves to ask what was wrong. He soon found them on top of a nearby hill. They were still singing their danger song and they all looked very upset.

Terry called out, "What is the problem?"

Wiley answered, "Something very bad is going to happen. We wolves can feel it in our bones." "Something bad? I don't feel a thing." Terry told Wiley.

"Young Wilbur was the first to feel that something is wrong, but now all of us wolves can feel it too."

"What is going to happen?" Terry asked.

Wiley answered, "We think an earthquake is about to happen."

"An earthquake?" Terry asked anxiously, "Are you sure?"

"I cannot be entirely certain, but I believe so. Oh, my, I think I can feel the first tremor," Wiley replied.

Just then Terry felt the earth move a bit under his tracks. Some small rocks shook loose and began to roll down the hill.

"My friends!" Terry cried. "They are in the cut. They may get buried by the falling rocks." He dashed down the hill to warn the others.

Terry ran into the cut shouting, "An earthquake is coming. Run for your lives."

The other machines looked up at Terry. At first they thought he was joking, but then they could see that he was quite serious.

Then they all felt the earth shaking. Small rocks began to tumble down on them. With Terry leading the way, Exeter, Timmy and Travis began to run out of the cut towards the fill.

The ground began to shake harder and larger rocks came tumbling down. Before they could get out of the cut, a huge landslide roared off the mountainside. The rocks blocked the way for the machines to escape.

They turned around to go back the other way but large rocks slammed into them. The landslide hit them and nearly buried the four machines. They could not move at all, held tight by the rocks.

Calib was on the fill, so he was not struck by the falling rocks or the landslide. He came as fast as he could towards his team members who were stuck in the landslide.

The earthquake was over and thick dust was rising. Calib made his way through the dust and over the rocks that had tumbled down the mountain into the cut. He got as close as possible to his teammates, and called out, "Are you okay?"

Timmy replied, "We can't move. The rocks and dirt are holding us fast. We all have some dents and broken headlights, but I don't think we are badly hurt. We just cannot move."

Just then Calib saw something very frightening. It was a large boulder on the hillside just above the trapped machines. The rock was beginning to slide down the hill toward the four machines. If the rock hit the machines, they would all be destroyed or at least badly damaged.

Calib acted immediately. He rushed up the hill towards the rock. Before he reached it, the rock broke free and began to roll very fast. Calib positioned himself right in front of the approaching rock. He was determined to save his teammates.

The rock hit Calib's bulldozer. His bulldozer
turned the rock, and it began to roll in another
direction. But Calib's bulldozer was smashed and
he was turned onto his side. Then Calib rolled
over down the hill. He rolled all the way over and
came back up on his steel wheels.

Calib had saved the other machines, but he was badly smashed and damaged.

The other machines were horrified. Terry called out, "Calib, are you still alive?"

Calib could hardly answer. "I'm really hurt badly. I'll need lots of repairs."

Just then the boss arrived. He could hardly
believe what had happened. He ran back to his
truck to phone for help. He called for machines
from another part of the job to come.

Soon an excavator named Elmer and a bulldozer tractor called Titus arrived and began to remove the rocks and dirt that held the machines.

Then a truck with lowboy trailer carried each machine to the workshop. Calib was the most badly damaged. His frame and his bulldozer were broken and had to be welded. His cab was smashed nearly flat so a new one was installed.

60

The other machines had less damage, just dents and broken headlights, so they were soon all properly repaired and back working on the job site.

In a few days Calib was repaired too. The truck brought him back to the job site.

When Terry saw Calib, he rushed up to him. He could hardly wait to tell his new compactor friend how much he appreciated what he had done for his fellow teammates. "You were awesome, Calib. None of your friends would have survived if you had not saved us."

The other machines agreed and thanked Calib, too. Just then Wiley and the wolf pack came by. Terry told the others how Wiley had warned him about the earthquake. All the machines then thanked the friendly wolves, as well.

Terry said, "I have learned a lot about teamwork from both Calib and Wiley. Being a good teammate is one of the most important things in the world."

Wiley agreed. "The pups, Wilbur and Wilford, have learned a lot about getting along together, as well."

He called the two wolf pups to come forward, and they did so without nipping at each other.

"Tell the machines what you have learned about being team members," Wiley told the pups.

Wilbur said, "I learned that Wilford may be a better singer than I am, but I was one of the first to know the earthquake was coming."

"That's right," Wilford agreed. "Wilbur told me that he knew danger was coming and I was the first to start singing the warning song."

Wiley said, "I am proud of both of these pups. They have learned to be good team members."

Everyone agreed that lessons in teamwork had been learned by both the machines and the wolves. So Wiley told them all, "Here is a team song we can all sing."

And the clever wolf taught the machines a new song about working as a team. There were yips and howls from the wolves. There were horns beeping and engines revving from the machines, but they all sang the song with exuberance.

Working as a team is fun
We each have a job to do
For even if we don't like everyone
Working together pulls us through.

WORKING AS A TEAM IS FUN
WE EACH HAVE A JOB TO DO
FOR EVEN IF WE DON'T LIKE EVERYONE
WORKING TOGETHER PULLS US THROUGH

WORKING TOGETHER SONG

This book is dedicated to devoted Terry fans Zack (left) and Drew, the grandsons of Bob Burchett illustrator of the Terry books. They are very "attached" to their grandfather, as you can see.

Mike Rucker

I was delighted when Mike told me that he would like to dedicate this book to my grandsons, Drew and Zack. They have been "Terry fans" from an early age.

Bob Burchett

The Illustrator

My family did not have a television as I was growing up. We "watched" a radio as we listened to the great radio programs of the day and made up our own pictures in our head.

When not involved in my career as a graphic illustrator one of my passions is still old time radio. I have been involved with the Old Time Radio Convention since 1978. This photo was taken at the 30th Annual Old Time Radio Convention in Newark, New Jersey October, 2005.

During these annual conventions some stars of the old shows attend and are surprised that they were still fondly remembered. Many of them did not have recordings of their shows. Often the dealers in recordings of old radio shows will give the original radio actors copies of their own programs from fifty or more years ago. Sometimes the actors have told us that they had never even heard certain of their own shows until provided with these recordings. Almost all of them have stated that at the time of their star appearance on radio they never realized how good they had it.

Bob Burchett

Author's comments

My Terry the Tractor stories often involve a teamwork theme. Working together with others is important in most of life's endeavors. Most significant jobs, such as construction work, involve teamwork. In addition to the construction crew team, I also used a wolf pack in this story because even wolves must work together to be successful. Both Terry and the wolf cubs start off with some problems but learn to become good team members.

Humans (and perhaps machines and wolves) will always probably have a few problems getting along with one another, but as Terry's boss says, "The mark of a great team is not that all the players are compatible. The important thing is how well they handle incompatibility."

A final word about the wolves: it is well established that some animals can anticipate that an earthquake is coming and that seems to fit well into this story, as well.

Books in the Terry the Tractor series
by Mike Rucker

Terry the Tractor
Terry and the Bully
Terry the Athlete
Terry and the Super Powerful Fuel
Terry and the Elephant
Terry and the Ecological Disaster
Terry and the High-Tech Laser Guided, Satellite Transmitted, Dozing System
Terry and the South Pole Breakdown
Terry the Smoke Jumper
Terry and the Wild Well Blowout
Terry and the Beaver Dam Fiasco
Terry and the Trouble with Trash
Terry and the Obsolete Locomotive
Terry and the Earthquake

Coming Soon:

Terry and the Martians

To order any of the Terry the Tractor books, send a check for $5.95 (includes postage) for each title to:

Mike Rucker
1003 W. Centennial Dr.
Peoria, IL 61614-2828

Or, visit Terry on the worldwide web at: **www.terrythetractor.com**